ARTHUR'S
GREAT BIG
VALENTINE

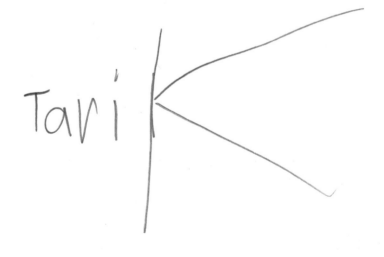

Tarik

An I Can Read Book®

ARTHUR'S GREAT BIG VALENTINE

Story and Pictures by
LILLIAN HOBAN

HarperCollins*Publishers*

HarperCollins®, 🏠®, and I Can Read Book®
are trademarks of HarperCollins Publishers Inc.

17 18 19 20 SCP 20 19 18

Library of Congress Cataloging-in-Publication Data
Hoban, Lillian.
    Arthur's great big valentine / by Lillian Hoban. — 1st ed.
        p.   cm. — (An I can read book)
    Summary: After they have a falling out, Arthur and his best friend
Norman make up with very special valentines.
    ISBN 0-06-022406-1 :   ISBN 0-06-022407-X (lib. bdg.) :
ISBN 0-06-444149-0 (pbk.)
    [1. Friendship—Fiction.   2. Valentine's Day—Fiction.]
I. Title.   II. Series.
PZ7.H635Arg 1989   88-21202
[E]—dc19   CIP

For Ben,

my best valentine

It was a snowy Valentine's day.

Arthur was getting ready to go out.

He put on his boots and his scarf.

He put on his hat and his mittens.

Violet was making valentines.

She drew red and yellow flowers

and big red hearts.

"I am making ten valentines,"

she said,

"five for my best friends

and five for my not-so-best friends.

How many are you making, Arthur?"

"None," said Arthur.

"I don't have any best friends."

"I thought Norman

was your best friend," said Violet.

"He was," said Arthur.

"But he got mad when I played Tarzan.

I was swinging from the branch

where he was sitting.

The branch broke, and he fell down

and ripped his new jacket.

Now he has a secret club,

and he will not let me be in it."

"You could make valentines
for your not-so-best friends,"
said Violet.

"All of my not-so-best friends
are in Norman's secret club,"
said Arthur.

"I think I will go have
a snowball fight by myself."

"You can't have a snowball fight
by yourself," said Violet.

"Yes I can," said Arthur.

"Watch me."

Arthur went outside.

He made a snowball

and threw it high in the air.

Then he ran fast

so he would be under the snowball

when it came down.

But he did not run fast enough.

The snowball came down *SPLAT!*
right in front of him.

"Well," said Arthur,

"lots of times I am under it

when it comes down.

So I *can* have a snowball fight

by myself."

"I will have a snowball fight
with you," said Violet.

"I will be your friend."

"Little sisters
can't be your friend,"
said Arthur.

"They cry if a snowball
hits them."

"I promise not to cry
if you promise not to pack
your snowballs too hard,"
said Violet.

"Okay," said Arthur. "I promise."

Violet ran to get her coat and hat
and mittens and boots.

Arthur practiced hitting himself
with snowballs.

15

He threw a snowball up high

and ran very fast.

But when the snowball came down,

Arthur was not under it.

Wilma was coming down the path,
and Wilma was under it.
SPLAT! The snowball landed
right on Wilma's head.

"That was not very nice, Arthur,"
said Wilma.

"I came over to invite you and Violet
to my valentine party.

But maybe I will just invite Violet."

"I don't care," said Arthur.

"Who else is coming to your party?"

18

"Norman and his little brother Tony,"
said Wilma. "And Peter and John
and Sally and Tessa."

"Then I would not come anyway,"
said Arthur.

"Wilma," called Violet.

"Do you want to have a snowball fight
with me and Arthur?"

"I can't," said Wilma.

"I am giving out invitations

to my valentine party."

She gave Violet a big red heart.

It said: MY VALENTINE PARTY.

It had a blue balloon pasted on it.

Inside there was a picture

of pink-frosted cookies

and little heart-shaped candies

in vanilla ice cream.

Underneath the picture it said:

The candy is red,
the balloons are blue.
It will be a great party
if you can come too!

Arthur looked at the picture.

Then he made another snowball.

"Where is Arthur's invitation?"

asked Violet.

"I do not want one,"

said Arthur quickly.

"Norman is coming to the party,

so I can't."

"That is a shame," said Wilma.

"We are having cinnamon candy

and pink-frosted cookies

and vanilla ice cream

and hot chocolate.

You should make up with Norman."

"Norman will not speak to me,"

said Arthur.

"I can't make up with him."

"You should give Norman

a valentine," said Wilma.

"Then you could be friends again."

24

"I made ten valentines,"
Violet said to Wilma.
"The best one is for you,
because you are my best friend.
I will bring it to the party."
"Can I see the other valentines?"
asked Wilma.
"Okay," said Violet.

Violet and Wilma

started toward the house.

"Hey!" yelled Arthur.

"I thought we were having

a snowball fight!"

"I will be back soon,"

called Violet.

"Phooey!" said Arthur.

"Little sisters are no fun."

Arthur sat down.

He drew a heart in the snow.

27

Inside the heart he wrote:
Violet
You are no fun,
and this is true—
if I had a friend
it would not be you!

"Hey, Arthur," called Peter.

"Is Violet at home?"

Peter was pulling a sled.

On the sled there was a box.

Inside the box

there were big and little envelopes.

"What are those?" asked Arthur.

"Valentines," said Peter.

"I made a whole bunch

that I am selling.

I deliver for free

if you buy one.

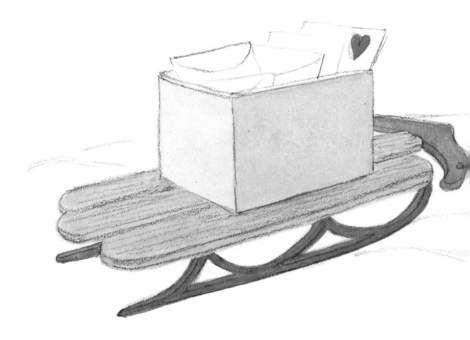

I have a whole stack

to deliver to Violet."

Peter looked in the box.

He pulled out all the envelopes

that were marked "Violet."

"Are there any for me?"

asked Arthur.

Peter looked in the box again.

"Nope," he said, "not one.

But you could buy some

and send them to yourself.

Here, these are two for 25¢."

Peter took out a valentine

and showed it to Arthur.

It was a heart-shaped flower
with a picture of a bee on it.
It said:

*Bee my valentine
and I will call you honey!*

"Pretty cute, isn't it?" said Peter.

"You could send a couple of these
to yourself."

"I am not sending any valentines
to myself!" yelled Arthur.

"Okay, okay," said Peter.

"I just thought

you might like to get one."

Peter went to deliver

Violet's valentines.

Arthur sat down again.

He drew another heart in the snow.

Inside the heart he wrote:

Valentines are stupid.

Some people get many.

I don't care

if I never get any.

PLOP! Some snow

trickled down Arthur's neck.

Someone bumped against his back

and tumbled over him.

It was Norman's little brother Tony.

"Hey!" yelled Arthur.

"Why don't you watch
where you are going?"

"I am sorry, Arthur," said Tony.

"I did not see you
because I was walking backward."

"Well, turn around

and walk frontward!" yelled Arthur.

"I can't," said Tony.

"I am making backward tracks

in the snow to trick Norman

so he will think

I went the other way."

Arthur looked at Tony's tracks.

"That is pretty neat,"

he said.

"It does look like you went

the other way.

Why do you want to trick Norman?"

"Because he made a secret valentine, and I know the secret," said Tony. "Now he is after me so I will not tell before he delivers it."

"Who is Norman's valentine for?"

asked Arthur.

"I will tell you

if you promise not to tell Norman

I told," said Tony.

"That is easy," said Arthur.

"I never tell Norman

anything anymore."

"Do you promise?" asked Tony.

"I promise," said Arthur.

"Cross your heart and hope to die?"

asked Tony.

"Cross my heart and hope to die,"

said Arthur.

"Okay," said Tony,

and he whispered something

in Arthur's ear.

Arthur opened his eyes very wide.

"Do you mean it?" he asked.

"You promised not to tell,"
said Tony.

"Oh boy! Oh boy!" said Arthur.

"I have to do something

about this fast!"

Arthur started to walk away.

"You promised!" yelled Tony.

"Cross your heart and hope to die."

"I know," said Arthur,

"and I am not telling."

"Then where are you going?"

asked Tony.

"I am not going anywhere,"

said Arthur.

"I am just making tracks in the snow.

Watch me."

Violet and Wilma came outside.

"What are you doing, Arthur?"

called Wilma.

"He is making tracks in the snow,"

said Tony.

"Arthur is making a big heart
with his tracks," said Violet.
"He is making a valentine!"

Arthur made a big heart

in the snow.

Inside the heart he

wrote a poem.

Just as Arthur finished,

Norman came down the path.

He was holding a big white envelope.

When he saw Arthur's valentine,

he stopped and read it.

You are my pal
and my buddy, too.
Please be my friend, Norman—
I really miss you!

55

"Do you really mean it, Arthur?"
he asked.

"I really mean it," said Arthur.

"Well," said Norman,

"I have a valentine for you, too."

Norman gave Arthur the envelope.

Inside there was a big red heart.

On the heart there was a picture

of red and blue flowers.

Under the picture it said:

Arthur
Roses are red,
Violets are blue.
I wish we were friends again—
there is no one like you!

"Oh boy!" said Arthur. "Oh boy!"

"Now Arthur can come

to the valentine party," said Violet.

"That's right," said Wilma,

"if he promises not to throw

any more snowballs at me."

"But Arthur promised

to have a snowball fight with *me*,"

said Violet.

Arthur looked at Norman.

Norman looked at Arthur.

"Let's go, buddy," yelled Arthur.

"Come on, pal!" yelled Norman.

"Me too! Me too!" shouted Tony.

"I get first shot!" called Violet.

She made a big snowball

and threw it.

It landed *SPLAT!* on Arthur's head.

So they all had a big snowball fight,

and Wilma joined in too.

Then they went
to Wilma's valentine party.
They had ice cream and
cinnamon candy and frosted cookies
and hot chocolate.

"This is my best Valentine's day,"
said Arthur.
He made a big heart
with the cinnamon candies
in his vanilla ice cream.

And inside the heart he wrote:

FRIENDS